Where Is My Little Joey?

Where Is My Little Joey?

By Donna Lugg Pape

Drawings by Tom Eaton

GARRARD PUBLISHING COMPANY
CHAMPAIGN, ILLINOIS

871284

Where Is My Little Joey?

Kara Kangaroo hopped
into the park.
She looked around.
Then she looked down
at her little Joey.
He was in her pocket
fast asleep.

Kara saw some mothers
with their babies.
The babies
were very quiet.

"Those babies
must be sleeping too,"
Kara thought.

Then she saw
that one of the mothers
was taking a nap.
"I'm tired,"
Kara said.
"I think
I'll take a nap too."
She closed her eyes
and went to sleep.

When Kara woke up,
she looked
in her pocket.
"My Joey is gone!"
she cried.
"Where could he be?"

"Joey! Joey!
Where are you?"
Kara hopped
around the park
looking for her baby.

"Joey! Joey!"
she called.
Then Kara hopped
out to the street.
She looked
up and down.
Some children
were playing
in the water.

She went
up to them.
"Have you seen
my Joey?"
she asked.

"No," said the children.
"We have not seen
your little Joey."
They went on playing
in the water.

Suddenly,
Kara's pocket
was full of water.

A bird flew down
and took a bath
in her pocket.
"Shoo! Shoo!"
Kara said.
"Get out of here!
My pocket
is not a bird bath!
My pocket
is for my little Joey."

Kara hopped
across the street
to the firehouse.

"I've lost
my little Joey,"
she told the firemen.
"I must find him.
Will you please
get this water
out of my pocket?"

Kara hopped on
down the street.
She stopped
to look for her Joey
in a store window.
"Could my Joey be here?"
she said.

While Kara was looking
in the window,
a man and a woman
came out of the store.
The woman saw Kara.

"What a good idea
for a planter,"
she said.
"This will look
very nice in my yard."
The man
put the plant
in Kara's pocket.
"Achoo! Achoo!"
said Kara.
She took the plant
out of her pocket.
She gave it back
to the man.

"I'm not a planter,"
Kara said.
And off she hopped
down the street.

"I must find my Joey,"
she said.
Kara saw some people
looking at something
in the park.

"Maybe they have found
my Joey!"
she thought.
But her Joey
was not there.
Instead,
she saw a monkey.
Kara stopped to watch
the monkey dance.
Then she felt something
in her pocket.
"My pocket
is not for money,"
Kara said.

She gave the money
to the man.
"My pocket
is for my Joey."
She hopped away.
"Where could
my Joey have gone?"

Kara thought to herself,
"I must find him!"
Kara looked and looked
for her Joey.
Then she saw
some children
playing ball.

Kara stopped
to watch them.
"Maybe they have seen
my Joey,"
she said.
She hopped over
to ask them.
Suddenly,
there was something
in her pocket.
Kara took the ball
out of her pocket.
She gave it back
to the children.

"My pocket
is not for balls,"
Kara told them.
"It is for my Joey.
I must find him."

Kara hopped away
once again.
By now
Kara was thirsty.
She stopped
for a drink of water.

While she was drinking,
children put some boxes
in Kara's pocket.

She took the boxes
and put them
in a litter basket.
"My pocket
is not for boxes,"
Kara said.

She hopped off again
to look for her Joey.
"I'm very tired,"
Kara said.
She stopped to rest.

She closed her eyes
and went to sleep.
Suddenly,
Kara felt something
in her pocket.

She opened her eyes.
"That's a funny mailbox,"
the child said.

Kara looked
in her pocket.
She took out the letter.

"My pocket
is not for letters.
It is
for my little Joey,"
she said.
"Where can he be?"
Kara hopped on.
Then she saw the mothers
with their babies.

"Maybe they have seen
my Joey.
I will ask them."
She hopped over
to the mothers.

"Have you seen my Joey?"
she asked.
"No, we haven't seen
your baby,"
they said.

Kara looked down
into a carriage.
"Joey!
Here is my Joey,"
she cried.

Kara hugged her baby.
She put him
in her pocket.

"My pocket
is not for plants
or money or balls.
It's not for boxes
or letters,"
Kara said happily.
"My pocket
is for my Joey!"

She looked down.
Once again
her Joey
was fast asleep.